Samuel Rogers

The Pleasures of Memory

Part I

Samuel Rogers

The Pleasures of Memory
Part I

ISBN/EAN: 9783744716208

Printed in Europe, USA, Canada, Australia, Japan

Cover: Foto ©Andreas Hilbeck / pixelio.de

More available books at **www.hansebooks.com**

THE

P L E A S U R E S

OF

M E M O R Y,

A   P O E M,

IN   TWO   PARTS.

BY THE AUTHOR OF

" AN ODE TO SUPERSTITION, WITH SOME OTHER POEMS."

Ampliat ætatis fpatium fibi bonus : hoc eft
Vivere bis, vitâ poffe priore frui.   MART.

L O N D O N:

PRINTED BY J. DAVIS.

SOLD BY T. CADELL, IN THE STRAND.

M DCC XCII.

THE

PLEASURES

OF

MEMORY.

PART I.

Dolce fentier,————— ——
Colle, che mi piacefti,———— ——
Ov' ancor per ufanza Amor mi mena;
Ben riconofco in voi l'ufate forme,
Non, laffo, in me.

PETRARCH.

A N A L Y S I S

FIRST PART.

THE Poem begins with the defcription of an obfcure village, and of the pleafing melancholy which it excites on being revifited after a long abfence. This mixed fenfation is an effect of the Memory. From an effect we naturally afcend to the caufe; and the fubject propofed is then unfolded with an inveftigation of the nature and leading principles of this faculty.

It is evident that there is a continued fucceffion of ideas in the mind, and that they introduce each other with a certain degree of regularity. Their complexion depends greatly on the different perceptions of plea-fure and pain which we receive through the medium of fenfe; and, in return, they have a confiderable influence on the animal economy.

They are fometimes excited by fenfible objects, and fometimes by an internal operation of the mind. Of the former fpecies is moft probably the memory of brutes; and its many fources of pleafure to them, as well as to ourfelves, are confidered in the firft part. The latter is the moft perfect degree of memory, and forms the fubject of the fecond.

When

When ideas have any relation whatever, they are attractive of each other in the mind; and the conception of any object naturally leads to the idea of another which was connected with it either in time or place, or which can be compared or contrasted with it. Hence arises our attachment to inanimate objects; hence also, in some degree, the love of our country, and the emotion with which we contemplate the celebrated scenes of antiquity. Hence a picture directs our thoughts to the original: and, as cold and darkness suggest forcibly the ideas of heat and light; he, who feels the infirmities of age, dwells most on whatever reminds him of the vigour and vivacity of his youth.

The associating principle, as here employed, is no less conducive to virtue than to happiness; and, as such, it frequently discovers itself in the most tumultuous scenes of life. It addresses our finer feelings, and gives exercise to every mild and generous propensity.

Not confined to man, it extends through all animated nature; and its effects are peculiarly striking in the domestic tribes.

THE

PLEASURES

OF

MEMORY.

PART I.

TWILIGHT's foft dews fteal o'er the village-green,

With magic tints to harmonize the fcene.

Hufh'd is the hum that thro' the hamlet broke,

When round the ruins of their ancient oak

The peafants flock'd to hear the minftrel play,

And games and carols clos'd the bufy day.

Her wheel at reſt, the matron charms no more

With treaſur'd tales of legendary lore.

All, all are fled ; nor mirth nor muſic flows,

To chaſe the dreams of innocent repoſe.   10

All, all are fled ; yet ſtill I linger here !

What penſive ſweets this ſilent ſpot endear ?

Mark yon old Manſion, frowning thro' the trees,

Whoſe hollow turret wooes the whiſtling breeze.

That caſement, arch'd with ivy's browneſt ſhade,   15

Firſt to theſe eyes the light of heav'n convey'd.

The mouldering gateway ſtrews the graſs-grown court,

Once the calm ſcene of many a ſimple ſport ;

When nature pleas'd, for life itſelf was new,

And the heart promis'd what the fancy drew.   20

See,

See, thro' the fractur'd pediment reveal'd,

Where mofs inlays the rudely-fculptur'd fhield,

The martin's old, hereditary neft,

Long may the ruin fpare its hallow'd gueft!

As jars the hinge, what fullen echoes call!   25

Oh hafte, unfold the hofpitable hall!

That hall, where once, in antiquated ftate,

The chair of juftice held the grave debate.

Now ftain'd with dews, with cobwebs darkly hung,

Oft has its roof with peals of rapture rung;   30

When round yon ample board, in due degree,

We fweeten'd every meal with focial glee.

The heart's light laughter crown'd the circling jeft;

And all was funfhine in each little breaft.

'Twas here we chas'd the flipper by its found;   35

And turn'd the blindfold hero round and round.

'Twas here, at eve, we form'd our fairy ring;

And Fancy flutter'd on her wildeft wing.

Giants and genii chain'd the wondering ear;

And orphan-woes drew Nature's ready tear.   40

Oft with the babes we wander'd in the wood,

Or view'd the foreft-feats of Robin Hood:

Oft, fancy-led, at midnight's fearful hour,

With ftartling ftep we fcal'd the lonely tow'r;

O'er infant innocence to hang and weep,   45

Murder'd by ruffian hands, when fmiling in its fleep.

   Ye Houfehold Deities! whofe guardian eye [1]

Mark'd each pure thought, ere regifter'd on high;

Still

Still, ſtill ye walk the conſecrated ground,

And breathe the ſoul of Inſpiration round.   50

  As o'er the duſky furniture I bend,

Each chair awakes the feeliugs of a friend.

The ſtoried arras, ſource of fond delight,

With old achievement charms the wilder'd ſight ;

And ſtill, with Heraldry's rich hues impreſt,   55

On the dim window glows the pictur'd creſt.

The ſcreen unfolds its many-colour'd chart.

The clock ſtill points its moral to the heart.

That faithful monitor 'twas heav'n to hear !

When ſoft it ſpoke a promis'd pleaſure near :   60

And has its ſober hand, its ſimple chime,

Forgot to trace the feather'd feet of Time ?

                                   That

That maffive beam, with curious carvings wrought,

Whence the caged linnet footh'd my penfive thought;

Thofe mufkets cas'd with venerable ruft;   65

Thofe once-lov'd forms, ftill breathing thro' their duft,

Still from the frame, in mould gigantic caft,

Starting to life—all whifper of the paft !

As thro' the garden's defert paths I rove,

What fond illufions fwarm in every grove !   70

How oft, when purple evening ting'd the weft,

We watch'd the emmet to her grainy neft;

Welcom'd the wild-bee home on wearied wing,

Laden with fweets, the choiceft of the fpring !

How oft infcrib'd, with Friendfhip's votive rhyme,   75

The bark now filver'd by the touch of Time;

Soar'd

Soar'd in the fwing, half pleas'd and half afraid,

Thro' fifter elms that wav'd their fummer fhade;

Or ftrew'd with crumbs yon root-inwoven feat,

To lure the redbreaft from his lone retreat !   80

Childhood's lov'd group revifits every fcene,

The tangled wood-walk and the tufted green !

Indulgent MEMORY wakes, and, lo ! they live !

Cloth'd with far fofter hues than Light can give.

Thou laft beft friend that Heav'n affigns below,   85

To footh and fweeten all the cares we know ;

Whofe glad fuggeftions ftill each vain alarm,

When nature fades, and life forgets to charm ;

Thee would the Mufe invoke !—to thee belong

The fage's precept, and the poet's fong.   90

What

What foften'd views thy magic glafs reveals,

When o'er the landfcape Time's meek twilight fteals !

As when in ocean finks the orb of day,

Long on the wave reflected luftres play ;

Thy temper'd gleams of happinefs refign'd   95

Glance on the darken'd mirror of the mind.

The School's lone porch, with reverend moffes gray,

Juft tells the penfive pilgrim where it lay.

Mute is the bell that rung at peep of dawn,

Quick'ning my truant-feet acrofs the lawn ;   100

Unheard the fhout that rent the noontide air,

When the flow dial gave a paufe to care.

Up fprings, at every ftep, to claim a tear,

Some little friendfhip form'd and cherifh'd here !

And

And not the lighteſt leaf, but trembling teems   105

With golden viſions, and romantic dreams!

    Down by yon hazel copſe, at evening, blaz'd

The Gipſy's faggot—there we ſtood and gaz'd;

Gaz'd on her ſun-burnt face with ſilent awe,

Her tatter'd mantle, and her hood of ſtraw;   110

Her moving lips, her caldron brimming o'er;

The drowſy brood that on her back ſhe bore;

Imps, in the barn, with mouſing owlet bred,

From rifled rooſt at nightly revel fed;

Whoſe dark eyes flaſh'd thro' locks of blackeſt ſhade,   115

When in the breeze the diſtant watch-dog bay'd:

And heroes fled the Sybil's mutter'd call,

Whoſe elfin prowefs ſcal'd the orchard-wall.

       As

As o'er my palm the filver piece fhe drew,

And traced the line of life with fearching view,　　　120

How throbb'd my fluttering pulfe with hopes and fears,

To learn the colour of my future years!

　Ah, then, what honeft triumph flufh'd my breaft!

This truth once known—To blefs is to be bleft!

We led the bending beggar on his way;　　　125

(Bare were his feet, his treffes filver-gray)

Sooth'd the keen pangs his aged fpirit felt,

And on his tale with mute attention dwelt.

As in his fcrip we dropp'd our little ftore,

And wept aloud to think it was no more;　　　130

He breath'd his prayer, " Long may fuch goodnefs live !"

'Twas all he gave, 'twas all he had to give.

Hark,

But hark ! thro' thofe old firs, with fullen fwell,

The church-clock ftrikes ! ye tender fcenes, farewell !

It calls me hence, beneath their fhade, to trace   135

The few fond lines that Time may foon efface.

On yon gray ftone, that fronts the chancel-door,

Worn fmooth by bufy feet now feen no more;

Each eve we fhot the marble thro' the ring,

When the heart danc'd, and life was in its fpring;   140

Alas ! unconfcious of the kindred earth,

That faintly echoed to the voice of mirth.

The glow-worm loves her emerald light to fhed,

Where now the fexton refts his hoary head.

Oft

Oft, as he turn'd the greenfward with his fpade, 145

He lectur'd every youth that round him play'd;

And, calmly pointing where his fathers lay,

Rous'd him to rival each, the hero of his day.

Hufh, ye fond flutterings, hufh ! while here alone

I fearch the records of each mouldering ftone. 150

Guides of my life ! Inftructors of my youth !

Who firft unveil'd the hallow'd form of Truth ;

Whofe every word enlighten'd and endear'd ;

In age belov'd, in poverty rever'd ;

In Friendfhip's filent regifter ye live, 155

Nor afk the vain memorial Art can give.

But when the fons of peace and pleafure fleep,

When only Sorrow wakes, and wakes to weep ;

What

What fpells entrance my vifionary mind,

With fighs fo fweet, with raptures fo refin'd ? 160

Etherial Power ! whofe fmile, at noon of night,

Recals the far-fled fpirit of delight,

Inftils that mufing melancholy mood,

Which charms the wife, and elevates the good ;

Bleft MEMORY, hail ! Oh, grant my grateful verfe 165

To fing thy triumphs, and thy gifts rehearfe ;

Pierce the dark clouds that round thy empire roll,

And trace its airy precincts in the foul.

Lull'd in the countlefs chambers of the brain,

Our thoughts are link'd by many a hidden chain. 170

Awake but one, and lo, what myriads rife !

Each ftamps its image as the other flies !

Each,

Each, as the varied avenues of fenfe

Delight or forrow to the foul difpenfe,

Brightens or fades; yet all, with magic art,   175

Control the latent fibres of the heart.

As ftudious Profpero's myfterious fpell

Conven'd the fubject-fpirits to his cell;

Each, at thy call, advances or retires,

As judgment dictates, or the fcene infpires.   180

Each thrills the feat of fenfe, that facred fource,

Whence the fine nerves direct their mazy courfe,

And thro' the frame invifibly convey

The fubtle, quick vibrations as they play.

Survey the globe, each ruder realm explore;

From Reafon's fainteft ray to Newton foar.

2   What

What different spheres to human blifs affign'd!

What flow gradations in the fcale of mind!

Yet mark in each thefe myftic wonders wrought;

Oh mark the fleeplefs energies of thought!   190

   Th' adventurous boy, that afks his little fhare,

And hies from home, with many a goffip's prayer,

Turns on the neighbouring hill, once more to fee

The dear abode of peace and privacy;

And as he turns, the thatch among the trees,   195

The fmoke's blue wreaths afcending with the breeze,

The village-common fpotted white with fheep,

The churchyard yews round which his fathers fleep;

All roufe Reflection's fadly pleafing train,

And oft he looks and weeps, and looks again.

                               So,

So, when the daring fons of Science drew [2]

The mild TUPIA's firm yet fond adieu

To all his foul beft lov'd, fuch tears he fhed,

While each foft fcene of fummer beauty fled :

Long o'er the wave a wiftful look he caft,   205

Long watch'd the ftreaming fignal from the maft;

Till twilight's dewy tints deceiv'd his eye,

And fairy forefts fring'd the evening fky.

So Scotia's Queen, as flowly dawn'd the day, [3]

Rofe on her couch, and gaz'd her foul away.   210

Her eyes had blefs'd the beacon's glimmering height,

That faintly tipt the feathery furge with light;

But now the morn with orient hues pourtray'd

Each caftled cliff, and brown monaftic fhade :

All

All touch'd the talifman's refiftlefs fpring,   215

And lo, what bufy tribes were inftant on the wing !

  As kindred objects kindred thoughts excite ⁺,

Thefe, with magnetic virtue, foon unite.

And hence this fpot gives back the joys of youth,

Warm as the life, and with the mirror's truth.   220

Hence home-felt pleafure prompts the Patriot's figh ;

This makes him wifh to live, and " dare to die."

For this FOSCARI, whofe relentlefs fate ⁱ

Venice fhould blufh to hear the Mufe relate,

When exile wore his blooming years away,   225

To forrow's long foliloquies a prey,

When reafon, juftice, vainly urg'd his caufe ;

For this he rous'd her fanguinary laws ;

D

Glad

Glad to return, tho' Hope could grant no more,

And chains and torture hail'd him to the fhore.   230

And hence the charm hiftoric fcenes impart:

Hence Tiber awes, and Avon melts the heart.

Aërial forms, in Tempe's claffic vale,

Glance thro' the gloom, and whifper in the gale;

In wild Vauclufe with love and LAURA dwell,   235

And watch and weep in ELOISA's cell ⁶.

'Twas ever thus.   As now at VIRGIL's tomb ⁷,

We blefs the fhade, and bid the verdure bloom :

So TULLY paus'd, amid the wrecks of Time ⁸,

On the rude ftone to trace the truth fublime ;   240

When at his feet, in honour'd duft difclos'd,

Th' immortal Sage of Syracufe repos'd.

And

And as his youth in fweet delufion hung,

Where once a PLATO taught, a PINDAR fung;

Who now but meets him mufing, when he roves   245

His ruin'd Tufculan's romantic groves?

In Rome's great forum, who but hears him roll

His moral thunders o'er the fubject-foul?

And hence that calm delight the portrait gives:

We gaze on every feature till it lives!   250

Still the fond lover views the abfent maid;

And the loft friend ftill lingers in his fhade!

Say why the penfive widow loves to weep',

When on her knee fhe rocks her babe to fleep:

Tremblingly ftill, fhe lifts his veil to trace   255

The father's features in his infant face.

D 2

The

The hoary grandfire fmiles the hour away,

Won by the charm of Innocence at play;

He bends to catch each artlefs burft of joy,

Forgets his age, and acts again the boy.   260

What tho' the iron fchool of War erafe

Each milder virtue, and each fofter grace;

What tho' the fiend's torpedo-touch arreft

Each gentler, finer impulfe of the breaft;

Still fhall this active principle prefide,   265

And wake the tear to Pity's felf denied.

The intrepid Swifs, that guards a foreign fhore,

Condemn'd to climb his mountain-cliffs no more,

If chance he hear that fong fo fweetly wild ¹°,

His heart would fpring to hear it, when a child;   270

That

That fong, as fimple as the joys he knew,

When in the fhepherd-dance he blithely flew;

Melts at the long-loft fcenes that round him rife,

And finks a martyr to repentant fighs.

Afk not if courts or camps diffolve the charm;   275

Say why VESPASIAN lov'd his Sabine farm '';

Why great NAVARRE, when France and freedom bled '',

Sought the lone limits of a foreft-fhed.

When DIOCLETIAN's felf-corrected mind ''

Th' imperial fafces of a world refign'd,   280

Say why we trace the labours of his fpade,

In calm Salona's philofophic fhade.

Say, when ambitious CHARLES renounc'd a throne '',

To mufe with monks unletter'd and unknown,

                                                    What

What from his foul the parting tribute drew?   285

What claim'd the forrows of a laft adieu?

The ftill retreats that footh'd his tranquil breaft,

Ere grandeur dazzled, and its cares opprefs'd.

Undamp'd by time the generous Inftinct glows,

Far as Angola's fands, as Zembla's fnows;   290

Glows in the tiger's den, the ferpent's neft,

On every form of varied life impreft.

The focial tribes its choiceft influence hail :—

And when the drum beats brifkly in the gale,

The war-worn courfer charges at the found,   295

And with young vigour wheels the pafture round.

Oft has the aged tenant of the vale

Lean'd on his ftaff to lengthen out the tale;

Oft

Oft have his lips the grateful tribute breath'd,

From fire to fon with pious zeal bequeath'd.　　　　300

When o'er the blafted heath the day declin'd,

And on the fcath'd oak warr'd the winter wind;

When not a diftant taper's twinkling ray

Gleam'd o'er the furze to light him on his way;

When not a fheep-bell footh'd his liftening ear,　　　305

And the big rain-drops told the tempeft near;

Then did his horfe the homeward track defcry '',

The track that fhunn'd his fad enquiring eye;

And win each wavering purpofe to relent,

With warmth fo mild, fo gently violent,　　　　310

That his charm'd hand the carelefs rein refign'd,

And doubts and terrors vanifh'd from his mind.

Recal the traveller, whofe alter'd form

Has borne the buffet of the mountain-ftorm;

And who will firſt his fond impatience meet ?　　　315

His faithful dog's already at his feet !

Yes, tho' the porter ſpurn him from his door,

Tho' all, that knew him, know his face no more,

His faithful dog ſhall tell his joy to each,

With that mute eloquence which paſſes ſpeech.　　　320

And ſee, the maſter but returns to die !

Yet who ſhall bid the watchful ſervant fly ?

The blaſts of heav'n, the drenching dews of earth,

The wanton inſults of unfeeling mirth ;

Theſe, when to guard Misfortune's ſacred grave,　　　325

Will firm Fidelity exult to brave.

　　Led by what chart, tranſports the timid dove

The wreaths of conqueſt, or the vows of love ?

Say, thro' the clouds what compaſs points her flight ?

Monarchs have gaz'd, and nations bleſt the ſight.　　　330

2　　　　　　　　　　　　　　　　　　　　　　　Pile

Pile rocks on rocks, bid woods and mountains rife,

Eclipfe her native fhades, her native fkies;—

'Tis vain ! thro' Ether's pathlefs wilds fhe goes,

And lights at laft where all her cares repofe.

Sweet bird! thy truth fhall Harlem's walls atteft [16],   335

And unborn ages confecrate thy neft.

When with the filent energy of grief,

With looks that afk'd, yet dar'd not hope relief,

Want, with her babes, round generous Valour clung,

To wring the flow furrender from his tongue,   340

'Twas thine to animate her clofing eye ;

Alas ! 'twas thine perchance the firft to die,

Crufh'd by her meagre hand, when welcom'd from the fky.

Hark ! the bee winds her fmall but mellow horn [17],

Blithe to falute the funny fmile of morn.   345

E   O'er

O'er thymy downs fhe bends her bufy courfe,

And many a ftream allures her to its fource.

'Tis noon, 'tis night.   That eye fo finely wrought,

Beyond the fearch of fenfe, the foar of thought,

Now vainly afks the fcenes fhe left behind ;   350

Its orb fo full, its vifion fo confin'd !

Who guides the patient pilgrim to her cell ?

Who bids her foul with confcious triumph fwell?

With confcious truth, retrace the mazy clue

Of varied fcents, that charm'd her as fhe flew ?   355

Hail MEMORY, hail ! thy univerfal reign

Guards the leaft link of Being's glorious chain.

THE END OF THE FIRST BOOK.

THE

PLEASURES

OF

MEMORY.

PART II.

——Degli anni e de l'obblio nemica,
Delle cose custode, e dispensiera.

TASSO.

ANALYSIS

OF THE

SECOND PART.

THE Memory has hitherto acted only in fubfervience to the fenfes; and fo far man is not eminently diftinguifhed from other animals: but, with refpect to man, fhe has a higher province; and is often bufily employed, when excited by no external caufe whatever. She preferves, for his ufe, the treafures of art and fcience, hiftory and philofophy. She colours all the profpects of life: for ' we can only anticipate the future, by concluding what is poffible from what is paft.'

On her agency depends every effufion of the Fancy, whofe boldeft effort can only compound or tranfpofe, augment or diminifh the materials fhe has collected and retained.

When the firft emotions of defpair have fubfided, and forrow has foftened into melancholy, fhe amufes with a retrofpect of innocent pleafures, and infpires that noble confidence which refults from the confcioufnefs of having acted well.

When

When fleep has fufpended the organs of fenfe from their office, fhe not only fupplies the mind with images, but affifts in their combination. And even in madnefs itfelf, when the foul is refigned over to the tyranny of a diftempered imagination, fhe revives paft perceptions, and awakens that train of thought which was formerly moft familiar.

Nor are we pleafed only with a review of the brighter paffages of life ; events, the moft diftreffing in their immediate confequences, are often cherifhed in remembrance with a degree of enthufiafm.

But the world and its occupations give a mechanical impulfe to the paffions, which is not very favourable to the indulgence of this feeling. It is in a calm and well-regulated mind that the Memory is moft perfect ; and folitude is her beft fphere of action.

With this fentiment is introduced a Tale, illuftrative of her influence in folitude, ficknefs, and forrow. And the fubject having now been confidered, fo far as it relates to man and the animal world, the Poem concludes with a conjecture, that fuperior beings are bleft with a nobler exercife of this faculty.

THE

THE

PLEASURES

OF

MEMORY.

PART II.

SWEET MEMORY, wafted by thy gentle gale,

Oft up the tide of Time I turn my fail,

To view the fairy-haunts of long-loft hours,

Bleft with far greener fhades, far frefher flowers.

Ages and climes remote to Thee impart   5

What charms in Genius, and refines in Art;

Thee,

Thee, in whofe hand the keys of Science dwell,

The penfive portrefs of her holy cell;

Whofe conftant vigils chafe the chilling damp

Oblivion fteals upon her veftal-lamp.   10

The friends of Reafon, and the guides of Youth,

Whofe language breath'd the eloquence of Truth;

Whofe life, beyond preceptive wifdom, taught

The great in conduct, and the pure in thought;

Thefe ftill exift, by Thee to Fame confign'd,   15

Still fpeak and act, the models of mankind.

From Thee fweet Hope her airy colouring draws;

And Fancy's flights are fubject to thy laws.

From Thee that bofom-fpring of rapture flows,

Which only Virtue, tranquil Virtue, knows.   20

2   When

When Joy's bright fun has fhed his evening-ray,

And Hope's delufive meteors ceafe to play;

When clouds on clouds the fmiling profpect clofe,

Still thro' the ftorm thy ftar ferenely glows:

Like yon fair orb, fhe gilds the brow of night

With the mild magic of reflected light.

The beauteous maid, that bids the world adieu,

Oft of that world will fnatch a fond review;

Oft at the fhrine neglect her beads, to trace

Some focial fcene, fome dear familiar face;

Forgot, when firft a father's ftern controul

Chas'd the gay vifions of her opening foul:

And ere, with iron tongue, the vefper-bell

Burfts thro' the cyprefs-walk, the convent-cell,

F

Oft will her warm and wayward heart revive,   35

To love and joy ftill tremblingly alive;

The whifper'd vow, the chafte carefs prolong,

Weave the light dance, and fwell the choral fong;

With rapt ear drink th' enchanting ferenade;

And, as it melts along the moonlight glade,   40

To each foft note return as foft a figh,

And blefs the youth that bids her flumbers fly.

But not till Time has calm'd the ruffled breaft,

Are thefe fond dreams of happinefs confeft.

Not till the rufhing winds forget to rave,   45

Is heav'n's fweet fmile reflected on the wave.

From Guinea's coaft purfue the leffening fail,

And catch the founds that fadden every gale.

Tell,

Tell, if thou canft, the fum of forrows there;

Mark the fixt gaze, the wild and frenzied glare,   50

The racks of thought, and freezings of defpair!

But paufe not then—beyond the weftern wave,

Go, view the captive barter'd as a flave!

Cruſh'd till his high heroic fpirit bleeds,

And from his nervelefs frame indignantly recedes.   55

    Yet here, ev'n here, with pleafures long refign'd,

Lo! MEMORY burfts the twilight of the mind:

Her dear delufions footh his finking foul,

When the rude fcourge prefumes its bafe controul;

And o'er Futurity's blank page diffufe   60

The full reflection of their vivid hues.

'Tis but to die, and then, to weep no more,

Then will he wake on Congo's diftant fhore;

F 2   Beneath

Beneath his plantain's ancient fhade, renew

The fimple tranfports that with freedom flew ;   65

Catch the cool breeze that mufky Evening blows,

And quaff the palm's rich nectar as it glows ;

The oral tale of elder time rehearfe,

And chant the rude traditionary verfe ;

With thofe, the lov'd companions of his youth,   70

When life was luxury, and friendfhip truth.

Ah ! why fhould Virtue dread the frowns of Fate ?

Hers what no wealth can win, no power create !

A little world of clear and cloudlefs day,

Nor wreck'd by ftorms, nor moulder'd by decay ;   75

A world, with MEMORY's ceafelefs fun-fhine bleft,

The home of Happinefs, an honeft breaft.

But

But moſt we mark the wonders of her reign,

When Sleep has lock'd the ſenſes in her chain.

When ſober Judgment has her throne reſign'd,   80

She ſmiles away the chaos of the mind;

And as warm Fancy's bright Elyſium glows,

From Her each image ſprings, each colour flows.

She is the ſacred gueſt! th' immortal friend!

Oft ſeen o'er ſleeping Innocence to bend,   85

In that dead hour of night to Silence giv'n,

Whiſpering ſeraphic viſions of her heav'n.

When the blithe ſon of Savoy, roving round

With humble wares and pipe of merry ſound,

From his green vale and ſhelter'd cabin hies,   90

And ſcales the Alps to viſit foreign ſkies;

Tho'

Tho' far below the forked lightnings play,

And at his feet the thunder dies away ;

Oft, in the faddle rudely rock'd to fleep,

While his mule browzes on the dizzy fteep,

With MEMORY's aid, he fits at home, and fees

His children fport beneath their native trees,

And bends, to hear their cherub-voices call,

O'er the loud fury of the torrent's fall.

But can her fmile with gloomy Madnefs dwell ?

Say, can fhe chafe the horrors of his cell ?

Each fiery flight on Frenzy's wing reftrain,

And mould the coinage of the fever'd brain ?

Pafs but that grate, which fcarce a gleam fupplies,

There in the duft the wreck of Genius lies !

He whofe arrefting hand fublimely wrought

Each bold conception in the fphere of thought ;

Who from the quarried mafs, like PHIDIAS, drew

Forms ever fair, creations ever new !

But, as he fondly fnatch'd the wreath of Fame,   110

The fpectre Poverty unnerv'd his frame.

Cold was her grafp, a withering fcowl fhe wore ;

And Hope's foft energies were felt no more.

Yet ftill how fweet the foothings of his art '' !

From the cold ftone what bright ideas ftart !   115

Ev'n now he claims the amaranthine wreath,

With fcenes that glow, with images that breathe !

And whence thefe fcenes, thefe images, declare.

Whence but from Her who triumphs o'er defpair ?

Awake,

Awake, arife! with grateful fervour fraught,   120

Go, fpring the mine of elevated thought.

He who, thro' Nature's various walk, furveys

The good and fair her faultlefs line pourtrays;

Whofe mind, prophan'd by no unhallow'd gueft,

Culls from the crowd the pureft and the beft;   125

May range, at will, bright Fancy's golden clime,

Or, mufing, mount where Science fits fublime,

Or wake the fpirit of departed Time.

Who acts thus wifely, mark the moral mufe,

A blooming Eden in his life reviews!   130

So richly cultur'd every native grace,

Its fcanty limits he forgets to trace :

But the fond fool, when evening fhades the fky,

Turns but to ftart, and gazes but to figh !

The

The weary wafte, that lengthen'd as he ran,   135

Fades to a blank, and dwindles to a fpan!

Ah who can tell the triumphs of the mind,

By truth illumin'd, and by tafte refin'd?

When Age has quench'd the eye and clos'd the ear,

Still nerv'd for action in her native fphere,   140

Oft will fhe rife—with fearching glance purfue

Some long-lov'd image vanifh'd from her view;

Dart thro' the deep receffes of the paft,

O'er dufky forms in chains of flumber caft;

With giant-grafp fling back the folds of night,   145

And fnatch the faithlefs fugitive to light.

So thro' the grove th' impatient mother flies,

Each funlefs glade, each fecret pathway tries;

G   Till

Till the light leaves the truant-boy difclofe,

Long on the wood-mofs ftretch'd in fweet repofe.   150

   Nor yet to pleafing objects are confin'd

The filent feafts of the reflective mind.

Danger and death a dread delight infpire;

And the bald veteran glows with wonted fire,

When, richly bronz'd by many a fummer fun,   155

He counts his fcars, and tells what deeds were done.

   Go, with old Thames, view Chelfea's glorious pile;

And afk the fhatter'd hero, whence his fmile?

Go, view the fplendid domes of Greenwich, go;

And own what raptures from Reflection flow.   160

                          Hail,

Hail, nobleft ftru&tures imag'd in the wave !

A nation's grateful tribute to the brave.

Hail, bleft retreats from war and fhipwreck, hail !

That oft arreft the wondering ftranger's fail.

Long have ye heard the narratives of age,   165

The battle's havoc, and the tempeft's rage ;

Long have ye known Reflection's genial ray

Gild the calm clofe of Valour's various day.

Time's fombrous touches foon corre& the piece,

Mellow each tint, and bid each difcord ceafe :   170

A fofter tone of light pervades the whole,

And breathes a penfive languor o'er the foul.

Haft thou thro' Eden's wild-wood vales purfued ''

Each mountain-fcene, magnificently rude ;

To mark the fweet fimplicity of life,   175

Far from the din of Folly's idle ftrife:

Nor, with Attention's lifted eye, rever'd

That modeft ftone which pious PEMBROKE rear'd;

Which ftill records, beyond the pencil's power,

The filent forrows of a parting hour;   180

Still to the paufing pilgrim points the place,

Her fainted fpirit moft delights to trace?

   Thus, with the manly glow of honeft pride[10],

O'er his dead fon old ORMOND nobly figh'd.

Thus, thro' the gloom of SHENSTONE's fairy grove,   185

MARIA's urn ftill breathes the voice of love.

   As the ftern grandeur of a Gothic tower

Awes not fo deeply in its morning hour,

2   As

As when the fhades of Time ferenely fall

On every broken arch and ivied wall;   190

The tender images we love to trace,

Steal from each year ' a melancholy grace !'

And as the fparks of focial love expand,

As the heart opens in a foreign land;

And with a brother's warmth, a brother's fmile,   195

The ftranger greets each native of his ifle ;

So fcenes of life, when prefent and confeft,

Stamp but their bolder features on the breaft ;

Yet not an image, when remotely view'd,

However trivial, and however rude,   200

But wins the heart, and wakes the focial figh,

With every claim of clofe affinity !

But

But thefe pure joys the world can never know;

In gentler climes their filver currents flow.   205

Oft at the filent fhadowy clofe of day,

When the hufh'd grove has fung its parting lay;

When penfive Twilight, in her dufky car,

Slowly afcends to meet the evening-ftar;

Above, below, aërial murmurs fwell [21],   210

From hanging wood, brown heath, and bufhy dell!

A thoufand namelefs rills, that fhun the light,

Stealing foft mufic on the ear of night.

So oft the finer movements of the foul,

That fhun the fphere of Pleafure's gay controul,   215

In the ftill fhades of calm Seclufion rife,

And breathe their fweet feraphic harmonies!

Once,

Once, and domeſtic annals tell the time,

(Preferv'd in Cumbria's rude romantic clime)

When Nature fmil'd, and o'er the landſcape threw

Her richeſt fragrance, and her brighteſt hue,   220

A blithe and blooming Foreſter explor'd

Thoſe nobler ſcenes SALVATOR's foul ador'd;

The rocky paſs half hung with ſhaggy wood,

And the cleft oak flung boldly o'er the flood;

Eager to bid the mountain-echoes wake,   225

And ſhoot the wild-fowl of the ſilver lake.

High on exulting wing the heath-cock roſe,

And blew his ſhrill blaſt o'er perennial fnows;

When the rapt youth, recoiling from the roar,

Gaz'd on the tumbling tide of dread Lodoar;   230

And

And thro' the rifted cliffs, that fcal'd the fky,

Derwent's clear mirror charm'd his dazzled eye ".

Each ofier ifle, inverted on the wave,

Thro' morn's gray mift its melting colours gave;

And, o'er the cygnet's haunt, the mantling grove   235

Its emerald arch with wild luxuriance wove.

Light as the breeze that brufh'd the orient dew,

From rock to rock the young adventurer flew;

And day's laft funfhine flept along the fhore,

When, lo! an ambufh'd path the fmile of welcome wore.   240

Imbowering fhrubs with verdure veil'd the fky,

And on the mufk-rofe fhed a deeper dye;

Save when a mild and momentary gleam

Glanc'd from the white foam of fome fhelter'd ftream.

O'er

O'er the ftill lake the bell of evening toll'd,   245

And on the moor the fhepherd penn'd his fold;

And on the green hill's fide the meteor play'd,

When, hark ! a voice fung fweetly thro' the fhade.

It ceas'd—yet ftill in FLORIO's fancy fung,

Still on each note his captive fpirit hung ;   250

Till o'er the mead a cool fequefter'd grot

From its rich roof a fparry luftre fhot.

A cryftal water crofs'd the pebbled floor,

And on the front thefe fimple lines it bore :

     Hence away, nor dare intrude !   255

     In this fecret fhadowy cell

     Mufing MEMORY loves to dwell,

     With her fifter Solitude.

        H   Far

Far from the bufy world fhe flies,

To tafte that peace the world denies.   260

Entranc'd fhe fits; from youth to age,

Reviewing Life's eventful page;

And noting, ere they fade away,

The little lines of yefterday.

FLORIO had gain'd a rude and rocky feat,   265

When lo, the Genius of this ftill retreat!

Fair was her form—but who can hope to trace

The penfive foftnefs of her angel-face?

Can VIRGIL's verfe, can RAPHAEL's touch impart

Thofe finer features of the feeling heart,   270

Thofe tend'rer tints that fhun the carelefs eye,

And in the world's contagious circle die?

She left the cave, nor mark'd the ftranger there;

Her paftoral beauty, and her artlefs air,

Had breath'd a foft enchantment o'er his foul!   275

In every nerve he felt her bleft controul!

What pure and white-wing'd agents of the fky,

Who rule the fprings of facred fympathy,

Inform congenial fpirits when they meet?

Sweet is their office, as their nature fweet!   280

FLORIO, with fearful joy, purfued the maid,

Till thro' a vifta's moonlight-checquer'd fhade,

Where the bat circled, and the rooks repos'd,

(Their wars fufpended, and their counfels clos'd)

An antique manfion burft in awful ftate,   285

A rich vine cluftering round its Gothic gate.

H 2   Nor

Nor paus'd he here.   The mafter of the fcene

Mark'd his light ftep imprint the dewy green ;

And, flow-advancing, hail'd him as his gueft,

Won by the honeft warmth his looks exprefs'd.   290

He wore the ruftic manners of a 'Squire ;

Age had not quench'd one fpark of manly fire ;

But giant Gout had bound him in her chain,

And his heart panted for the chafe in vain.

Yet here Remembrance, fweetly-foothing power !   295

Wing'd with delight Confinement's lingering hour.

The fox's brufh ftill emulous to wear,

He fcour'd the county in his elbow-chair ;

And, with view-halloo, rous'd the dreaming hound,

That rung, by ftarts, his deep-ton'd mufic round.   300

Long by the paddock's humble pale confin'd,

His aged hunters cours'd the viewlefs wind :

And each, with glowing energy pourtray'd,

The far-fam'd triumphs of the field difplay'd ;

Ufurp'd the canvas of the crowded hall,   305

And chas'd a line of heroes from the wall.

There flept the horn each jocund echo knew,

And many a fmile, and many a ftory drew !

High o'er the hearth his foreft-trophies hung,

And their fantaftic branches wildly flung.   310

How would he dwell on each vaft antler there !

This dafh'd the wave, that fann'd the mountain-air.

Each, as it frown'd, unwritten records bore,

Of gallant feats and feftivals of yore.

But why the tale prolong?—His only child,   315

His darling JULIA on the ſtranger ſmil'd.

Her little arts a fretful ſire to pleaſe,

Her gentle gaiety, and native eaſe,

Had won his ſoul—but ah! few days had paſs'd,

Ere his fond viſions prov'd too ſweet to laſt.   320

When evening ting'd the lake's etherial blue,

And her deep ſhades irregularly threw ;

Their ſhifting ſail dropp'd gently from the cove,

Down by St. Herbert's conſecrated grove [13];

Whence erſt the chanted hymn, the taper'd rite,   325

Amus'd the fiſher's ſolitary night ;

And ſtill the mitred window, richly wreath'd,

A ſacred calm thro' the brown foliage breath'd.

The

The wild deer, ftarting thro' the filent glade,

With fearful gaze, their various courfe furvey'd.   330

High hung in air the hoary goat reclin'd,

His ftreaming beard the fport of every wind ;

And, as the coot her jet-wing lov'd to lave,

Rock'd on the bofom of the fleeplefs wave ;

The eagle rufh'd from Skiddaw's purple creft,   335

A cloud ftill brooding o'er her giant-neft.

And now the moon had dimm'd, with dewy ray,

The few fine flufhes of departing day ;

O'er the wide water's deep ferene fhe hung,

And her broad lights on every mountain flung ;   340

When lo ! a fudden blaft the veffel blew²⁴,

And to the furge confign'd its little crew.

All,

All, all efcap'd—but ere the lover bore

His faint and faded JULIA to the fhore,

Her fenfe had fled!—Exhaufted by the ftorm,   345

A fatal trance hung o'er her pallid form;

Her clofing eye a trembling luftre fir'd;

'Twas life's laft fpark—it flutter'd and expir'd!

The father ftrew'd his white hairs in the wind,

Call'd on his child—nor linger'd long behind: 350

And FLORIO liv'd to fee the willow wave,

With many an evening whifper, o'er their grave.

Yes, FLORIO liv'd—and ftill of each poffeft,

The father cherifh'd, and the maid carefs'd!

For ever would the fond enthufiaft rove,   355

With JULIA's, fpirit, thro' the fhadowy grove;

Gaze

Gaze with delight on every fcene fhe plann'd,

Kifs every flowret planted by her hand.

Ah ! ftill he traced her fteps along the glade,

When hazy hues and glimmering lights betray'd   360

Half-viewlefs forms ; ftill liften'd as the breeze

Heav'd its deep fobs among the aged trees ;

And at each paufe her melting accents caught,

In fweet delirium of romantic thought !

Dear was the grot that fhunn'd the blaze of day ;   365

She gave its fpars to fhoot a trembling ray.

The fpring, that bubbled from its inmoft cell,

Murmur'd of JULIA's virtues as it fell ;

And o'er the dripping mofs, the fretted ftone,

In FLORIO's ear breath'd language not its own.   370

Her charm around th' enchantrefs MEMORY threw,

A charm that fooths the mind, and fweetens too !

But is Her magic only felt below ?

Say, thro' what brighter realms fhe bids it flow ;

To what pure beings, in a nobler fphere ²⁵,   375

She yields delight but faintly imag'd here :

All that till now their rapt refearches knew,

Not call'd in flow fucceffion to review ;

But, as a landfcape meets the eye of day,

At once prefented to their glad furvey !   380

Each fcene of blifs reveal'd, fince chaos fled,

And dawning light its dazzling glories fpread ;

Each chain of wonders that fublimely glow'd,

Since firft Creation's choral anthem flow'd ;

Each ready flight, at Mercy's fmile divine,   385

To diftant worlds that undifcover'd fhine,

Full

Full on her tablet flings its living rays,

And all combin'd with bleft effulgence blaze.

There thy bright train, immortal Friendfhip, foar;

No more to part, to mingle tears no more! 390

And, as the foftening hand of Time endears

The joys and forrows of our infant-years,

So there the foul, releas'd from human ftrife,

Smiles at the little cares and ills of life;

Its lights and fhades, its funfhine and its fhowers; 395

As at a dream that charm'd her vacant hours!

Oft may the fpirits of the dead defcend,

To watch the filent flumbers of a friend;

To hover round his evening-walk unfeen,

And hold fweet converfe on the dufky green; 400

To

To hail the fpot where firft their friendfhip grew,

And heav'n and nature open'd to their view!

Oft, when he trims his cheerful hearth, and fees

A fmiling circle emulous to pleafe;

There may thefe gentle guefts delight to dwell,   405

And blefs the fcene they lov'd in life fo well!

Oh thou! with whom my heart was wont to fhare

From Reafon's dawn each pleafure and each care;

With whom, alas! I fondly hoped to know

The humble walks of happinefs below;   410

If thy bleft nature now unites above

An angel's pity with a brother's love,

Still o'er my life preferve thy mild controul,

Correct my views, and elevate my foul;

Grant me thy peace and purity of mind,   415

Devout yet cheerful, active yet refign'd;

Grant

Grant me, like thee, whofe heart knew no difguife,

Whofe blamelefs wifhes never aim'd to rife,

To meet the changes Time and Chance prefent,

With modeft dignity and calm content.   420

When thy laft breath, ere Nature funk to reft,

Thy meek fubmiffion to thy God exprefs'd ;

When thy laft look, ere thought and feeling fled,

A mingled gleam of hope and triumph fhed ;

What to thy foul its glad affurance gave,   425

Its hope in death, its triumph o'er the grave ?

The fweet Remembrance of unblemifh'd youth,

Th' infpiring voice of Innocence and Truth !

Hail, MEMORY, hail ! in thy exhauftlefs mine,

From age to age unnumber'd treafures fhine !   230

Thought and her fhadowy brood thy call obey,

And Place and Time are fubject to thy fway !

                                                          Thy

Thy pleasures most we feel, when most alone ;

The only pleasures we can call our own.

Lighter than air, Hope's summer-visions die,   435

If but a fleeting cloud obscure the sky ;

If but a beam of sober Reason play,

Lo, Fancy's fairy frost-work melts away !

But can the wiles of Art, the grasp of Power,

Snatch the rich relics of a well-spent hour ?   440

These, when the trembling spirit wings her flight,

Pour round her path a stream of living light ;

And gild those pure and perfect realms of rest,

Where Virtue triumphs, and her sons are blest !

THE END.

N O T E S.

FIRST PART.

───────

Note I. Verse 47.

Ye Household Deities, &c.

THESE were imagined to be the departed souls of virtuous men, who, as a reward of the good deeds they had performed in the present life, were appointed after death to the pleasing office of superintending the concerns of their respective descendants.

MELMOTH's Rem. on Cato, p. 287.

Note II. Verse 201.

So, when the daring sons of science, &c.

He wept; but the effort that he made to conceal his tears, concurred, with them, to do him honour: he went to the mast-head, &c.

HAWKESWORTH's Voyages, ii. 181.

Another very affecting instance of local attachment is related of his fellow-countryman Potaveri, who came to Europe with M. de Bougainville.　　　　　See LES JARDINS, chant. ii.

Note III. Verse 209.

So Scotia's Queen, &c.

Elle se leve sur son lict, & se mit à contempler la France encor, tant qu'elle peut.　　　　　BRANTÔME, tom. ii. p. 119.

Note IV. Verfe 217.

As kindred objects kindred thoughts excite,
Thefe, with magnetic virtue, foon unite.

To an accidental affociation may be afcribed fome of the nobleft efforts of human genius. The Hiftorian of the Decline and Fall of the Roman Empire firft conceived his defign among the ruins of the Capitol; and to the tones of a Welfh harp are we indebted for the Bard of Gray.   GIBBON's Hift. xii. 432. Memoirs of Gray, fect. iv. let. 25.

Note V. Verfe 223.

For this FOSCARI, &c.

This young man was fufpected of murder, and at Venice fufpicion is good evidence. Neither the intereft of the Doge his father, nor the intrepidity of confcious innocence which he exhibited in the dungeon and on the rack, could procure his acquittal. He was banifhed to the ifland of Candia for life.

But here his refolution failed him. At fuch a diftance from home he could not live; and as it was a criminal offence to folicit the inter-ceffion of any foreign prince, in a fit of defpair he addreffed a letter to the Duke of Milan, and intrufted it to a wretch whofe perfidy, he knew, would occafion his being remanded a prifoner to Venice.

See Dr. MOORE's View of Society in Italy, vol. i. let. 14.

Note VI. Verfe 236.

And watch and weep in ELOISA's cell.

The Paraclete, founded by Abelard, in Champagne.

NOTE

Note VII. Verse 237.

'Twas ever thus. As now at VIRGIL's tomb—

Vows and pilgrimages are not peculiar to the religious enthusiaſt. Silius Italicus performed annual ceremonies on the mountain of Poſi- lippo; and it was there that Boccaccio, *quaſi da un divino eſtro inſpirato*, reſolved to dedicate his life to the muſes.

Note VIII. Verse 239.

So TULLY paus'd amid the wrecks of Time.

When Cicero was quæſtor in Sicily, he diſcovered the tomb of Archi- medes by its mathematical inſcription.   Tuſc. Quæſt. 5. 3.

Note IX. Verse 253.

Say why the penſive widow loves to weep—

The influence of the aſſociating principle is finely exemplified in the faithful Penelope, when ſhe ſheds tears over the bow of Ulyſſes.

Od. xxi. 55.

Note X. Verse 269.

. If chance he hear that ſong ſo ſweetly wild—

The celebrated Ranz des Vaches; cet air ſi chéri des Suiſſes qu'il fut défendu ſous peine de mort de le jouer dans leurs troupes, parce qu'il faiſoit fondre en larmes, déſerter ou mourir ceux qui l'entendoient, tant il excitoit en eux l'ardent déſir de revoir leur pays.

Rousseau, Dictionnaire de Muſique.

K   Note

Note XI. Verfe 276.

Say why VESPASIAN lov'd his Sabine farm.

This emperor, according to Suetonius, conftantly paffed the fummer in a fmall villa near Reate, where he was born, and to which he would never add any embellifhment; *ne quid fcilicet oculorum confuetudini deperiret.*   Suet. in Vit. Vefp. cap. ii.

A fimilar inftance occurs in the life of the venerable Pertinax, as related by J. Capitolinus. Pofteaquam in Liguriam venit, multis agris coemptis, tabernam paternam, *manente forma priore,* infinitis ædificiis circundedit. Hift. Auguft. 54.

An attachment of this nature is generally the charaéteriftic of a benevolent mind; and a long acquaintance with the world cannot always extinguifh it.

To a friend, fays John Duke of Buckingham, I will expofe my weaknefs: I am oftener miffing a pretty gallery in the old houfe I pulled down, than pleafed with a faloon which I built in its ftead, though a thoufand times better in all refpeéts.—See his Letter to the D. of Sh.

This is the language of the heart; and will remind the reader of that good-humoured remark in one of Pope's letters—I fhould hardly care to have an old poft pulled up, that I remembered ever fince I was a child.   Pope's Works, viii. 151.

The elegant author of Telemachus has illuftrated this fubjeét, with equal fancy and feeling, in the ftory of Alibée, Perfan. See Recueil de Fables, compofées pour l'Education d'un Prince.

NOTE XII. Verſe 277.

Why great NAVARRE, &c.

That amiable and accompliſhed monarch, Henry the Fourth of France, made an excurſion from his camp, during the long ſiege of Laon, to dine at a houſe in the foreſt of Folambray ; where he had often been regaled, when a boy, with fruit, milk, and new cheeſe ; and in reviſiting which he promiſed himſelf great pleaſure.

Memoires de SULLY, tom. ii. p. 381.

NOTE XIII. Verſe 279.

When DIOCLETIAN's ſelf-correćted mind—

Diocletian retired into his native province, and there amuſed himſelf with building, planting, and gardening. GIBBON, ii. 175.

NOTE XIV. Verſe 283.

Say when ambitious CHARLES renounc'd a throne—

When the emperor Charles V. had executed his memorable reſolution, and had ſet out for the monaſtery of St. Juſtus, he ſtopped a few days at Ghent, ſays his hiſtorian, to indulge that tender and pleaſant melancholy, which ariſes in the mind of every man in the decline of life, on viſiting the place of his nativity, and viewing the ſcenes and objećts familiar to him in his early youth. ROBERTSON's Hiſt. iv. 256.

NOTE XV. Verſe 307.

Then did his horſe, &c.

The memory of the horſe forms the ground-work of a little pleaſing

K 2

romance

romance of the twelfth century, entitled "The Gray Palfrey." See the Tales of the Trouveurs, as collected by M. Le Grand.

Ariosto likewise introduces it in a passage full of truth and nature. When Bayardo meets Angelica in the forest,

———Va manfueto a la Donzella,

Ch' in Albracca il fervìa già di fua mano.

ORLANDO FURIOSO, canto i. 75.

NOTE XVI. Verfe 335.
Sweet bird ! thy truth fhall HARLEM's walls atteft.

During the fiege of Harlem, when that city was reduced to the laft extremity, and on the point of opening its gates to a bafe and barbarous enemy, a defign was formed to relieve it ; and the intelligence was conveyed to the citizens by a letter which was tied under the wing of a pigeon. THUANUS, lib. lv. c. 5.

The fame meffenger was employed at the fiege of Mutina, as we are informed by the elder Pliny. Hift. Nat. x. 37.

NOTE XVII. Verfe 344.
Hark ! the bee, &c.

This little animal, from the extreme convexity of her eye, cannot fee many inches before her.

NOTES

N O T E S

SECOND PART.

Note XVIII. Verfe 114.

Yet ftill how fweet the foothings of his art!

The aftronomer chalking his figures on the wall, in Hogarth's view of Bedlam, is an admirable exemplification of this idea.

See the Rake's Progress, plate 8.

Note XIX. Verfe 173.

Haft thou thro' Eden's wild-wood vales purfued, &c.

On the road-fide, between Penrith and Appelby, ftands a fmall pillar with this infcription:

"This pillar was erected in the year 1656, by Ann Countefs Dowager of Pembroke, &c. for a memorial of her laft parting, in this place, with her good and pious mother, Margaret, Countefs Dowager of Cumberland, on the 2d of April, 1616: in memory whereof fhe hath left an annuity of 4l. to be diftributed to the poor of the parifh of Brougham, every 2d day of April for ever, upon the ftone-table placed hard by. Laus Deo!"

The Eden is the principal river of Cumberland, and has its fource in the wildeft part of Weftmoreland.

Note

NOTE XX. Verſe 183.

Thus, with the manly glow of honeſt pride,
O'er his dead ſon old ORMOND nobly ſigh'd, &c.

Ormond bore the loſs with patience and dignity: though he ever retained a pleaſing, however melancholy, ſenſe of the ſignal merit of Oſſory. "I would not exchange my dead ſon," ſaid he, "for any living ſon in Chriſtendom." HUME, vi. 340.

The ſame ſentiment is inſcribed on Miſs Dolman's urn at the Lea-ſowes.

Heu, quanto minus eſt cum reliquis verſari, quam tui meminiſſe!

NOTE XXI. Verſe 210.

Above, below aërial murmurs ſwell.

At a diſtance were heard the murmurs of many waterfalls, not audi-ble in the day-time. GRAY, iv. 174.

NOTE XXII. Verſe 232.

Derwent's clear mirror.

The Lake of Keſwick in Cumberland.

NOTE XXIII. Verſe 324.

Down by St. Herbert's conſecrated grove.

A ſmall wooded iſland once dignified with a religious houſe.

NOTE XXIV. Verſe 341.

When lo! a ſudden blaſt the veſſel blew.

In a lake, ſurrounded with mountains, the agitations are often vio-lent and momentary. The winds blow in guſts and eddies; and the water no ſooner ſwells, than it ſubſides.

See BOURN's Hiſt. of Weſtmoreland.

2 NOTE

NOTE XXV. Verſe 375.

To what pure beings, in a nobler ſphere,
She yields delight but faintly imag'd here.

The ſeveral degrees of angels may probably have larger views, and ſome of them be endowed with capacities able to retain together, and conſtantly ſet before them, as in one picture, all their paſt knowledge at once.　　　LOCKE on Human Underſtanding, book ii. chap. x. 9.

F I N I S.